This edition published specially for Barnes & Noble, Inc. 2009 by Candlewick Press

Library of Congress Cataloging-in-Publication Data is available.

Library of Congress Catalog Card Number 2003040982 (*Sock Monkey Goes to Hollywood*)
Library of Congress Catalog Card Number 2003069564 (*Sock Monkey Boogie-Woogie*)

ISBN 978-0-7636-1962-6 (Candlewick trade edition. *Sock Monkey Goes to Hollywood*)
ISBN 978-0-7636-2392-0 (Candlewick trade edition. *Sock Monkey Boogie-Woogie*)

ISBN 978-1-4351-1950-5 (Barnes & Noble edition)
ISBN 978-0-7636-4724-7 (Candlewick edition)

10 11 12 13 14 15 SWT 10 9 8 7 6 5 4 3 2

Printed in Dongguan, Guangdong, China

This book was typeset in Cafeteria.
The illustrations were created digitally.

Candlewick Press
99 Dover Street
Somerville, Massachusetts 02144

visit us at www.candlewick.com

Sock Monkey
in the Spotlight

Cece Bell

CANDLEWICK PRESS

SOCK MONKEY
GOES TO
HOLLYWOOD

A Star Is Bathed

For Tom, and in memory of Henry

One day, Sock Monkey, the famous actor,
received a special delivery.

It was an invitation to attend the Oswald Awards! He was a nominee for Best Supporting Toy in a motion picture!

YiPPee!

Sock Monkey hopped with excitement.

But as he read on, the last words on the invitation made him gasp.

Once, long ago, Sock Monkey had been a spotless monkey. His whites were like the purest snow, his reds like the ripest apples, and his browns like a freshly pressed suit.

But Sock Monkey had been very active over the years . . .

and he had never, not once in his life, ever taken a bath.
Never. Now he was downright filthy.

Just thinking about taking a bath made Sock Monkey dizzy with fear.

A bath? Oh, no!

The stinky soap! The icy water! The scratchy towels!

A BATH WILL MAKE ME NOTHING MORE THAN A BLOTCHY, LUMPY, SHRUNKEN MONKEY!

But what if Sock Monkey won the Oswald and he wasn't there to accept it?

He had no choice. He *had* to get clean. So Sock Monkey turned to his friends for help.

Will you help me?

Certainly!

Of course!

What are friends for?

"The first step," said Miss Bunn, "is to be gently hand-washed in warm soapy water."

So Miss Bunn flew Sock Monkey to the warm Simian Springs, in the Mystical Monkey Mountains . . .

where a group of wild bathing monkeys carefully
washed him with a very mild soap.

"The next step," said Froggie, "is to rinse out all the soap with clear cool water."

So Froggie rowed Sock Monkey to the middle of the perfectly pure Lilypad Pond . . .

and Sock Monkey rinsed out all the soap by
swimming a few laps in the clear cool water.

"The final step," said Blue Pig, "is to lie on a soft fluffy towel for a good long while, until you are dry."

So Blue Pig drove Sock Monkey to the hot Sahara Sands . . .

and Sock Monkey basked all day in the sizzling sunshine.

At last, Sock Monkey was washed and dry. His friends could hardly wait to see his new look . . .

Now Sock Monkey could attend the awards show . . . and maybe win an Oswald!

Sock Monkey rented a tuxedo, and his friends helped him get ready for his big night.

Then a limo came and picked him up.

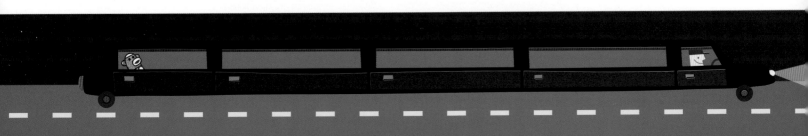

Sock Monkey couldn't believe he was finally there —
the Oswald Awards at the Big Theater!

He glided down the red carpet, while the other toys
greeted him with exclamations of astonishment.

Miss Bunn, Froggie, and Blue Pig watched the show on TV at home.

Sock Monkey looked nervous.

When the big moment finally arrived, Sock Monkey was ready to burst.

"AND THE NOMINEES ARE...

TEDDY BEAR
"KIDS, I SHRUNK THE HONEY"

TEDDY BEAR!

SOCK MONKEY
"DIRTY LARRY"

SOCK MONKEY!

JACK-IN-THE-BOX
"THE BOX AND THE HOUND"

BABY DOLL
"CHARLOTTE'S WET"

JACK-IN-THE-BOX!

BABY DOLL!

Who would win the Oswald?

"AND THE OSWALD FOR BEST SUPPORTING
TOY IN A MOTION PICTURE GOES TO . . .

JACK-in-THE-BOX!

Yippee!

Sigh

Boo-Hoo

Grrr!

Sock Monkey was disappointed. He watched in envy as
Jack accepted his Oswald.

But Sock Monkey was feeling fresh and clean — and
Jack really was a talented actor. So Sock Monkey decided
right then and there to celebrate Jack's success.

He was chatting with a famous actress and relishing a tasty bit of cheese when he heard another announcement:

THE ICHABOD THALBURG AWARD FOR CLEANEST NOMINEE GOES TO . . .

The crowd went wild.

Sock Monkey bounced up to the stage, feeling prouder
and cleaner than he had ever felt in his whole life.

TOOT   TOOT

"I'd like to thank the judges," said Sock Monkey as he accepted his very own Oswald.

"And give a special thank-you to my best friends — Miss Bunn, Froggie, and Blue Pig. I couldn't have done it without them."

THE END

SOCK MONKEY BOOGIE-WOOGIE

A Friend Is Made

For Granny Bell, Mary Ann,
and Sarah

Sock Monkey, the famous toy actor, was going to the Big Celebrity Dance, and he just couldn't wait.

But there was one problem. He needed a dance partner.

He'd ask Blue Pig, but he was going on a business trip.

He'd ask Froggie, but he was visiting family.

And he'd ask Miss Bunn, but she was taking a vacation.

All his friends were leaving!

Don't worry—
you'll find a
dance partner!

The next day, Sock Monkey was lonesome . . .

and he still didn't know what to do about the big dance.

So Sock Monkey decided to find a dance partner on his own. He put up a big sign, and he waited.

He didn't have to wait long.

WANTED:
GOOD
DANCeR
to dance with
Sock Monkey
(famous actor)
at the
BIG CeLeBRITY
DANCE!

Just about every toy in town responded to Sock Monkey's sign.

Too tall!

Too small!

Too dizzy!

Too busy!

Unfortunately, the auditions did not go so well.

Too clunky!

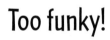

Too funky!

Bad breath.

What was Sock Monkey going to do?
Just when he felt nothing could go right,
three packages arrived.

They were gifts from his friends!

Miss Bunn gave him a beautiful hat and sweater,
Blue Pig mailed a pair of enormous socks, and
Froggie sent cotton from his family's farm.

As Sock Monkey admired his gifts, a wonderful idea began to form in his head.

AHA!

He knew exactly what to do!

The first thing Sock Monkey did was cut the buttons off his new sweater . . .

and he unraveled it until he had a big ball of yarn.

Next he turned the socks inside out. Then he cut . . .

and he sewed them with the yarn . . .

and he stuffed everything with cotton . . .

until at last, he had finished his masterpiece.

Sock Monkey had made another monkey . . .

HELLO!
I AM SOCK BUDDY!
I CAN MAKE CUPCAKES!

and maybe the perfect dance partner!

Sock Monkey couldn't believe his luck — Sock Buddy was
a fast learner. He could really shimmy!

When Sock Monkey and Sock Buddy were finally on their way to the Big Celebrity Dance, they could hardly hide their excitement.

They pulled up to the dance club in Sock Monkey's fancy new convertible.

The doorman was impressed.

Inside, Sock Monkey was interviewed for TV, and he proudly presented his dance partner to the whole world.

Sock Buddy had never seen so many toys before.
He wanted to run to the nearest exit.

At first, Sock Monkey and
Sock Buddy had a little
trouble warming up.

But soon, they remembered all the boogie-woogie moves they'd practiced.

The dance was amazing — and over all too soon.
On the way home, Sock Monkey told Sock Buddy that
tomorrow was another big day. Miss Bunn, Blue Pig, and
Froggie would be coming home!

And when—at last—his friends returned, Sock Monkey was thrilled to see them again.

When Sock Monkey introduced Miss Bunn, Froggie, and Blue Pig to Sock Buddy, they liked him right away.

They felt as if they had known him forever.

THE END